THE RIVER GODDESS
A PREQUEL

PUNITA RICE

RISING GRAINS PUBLISHING

First Edition

Rice, Punita C.

The River Goddess: A Prequel / Punita Rice. — 1st ed.

Summary: When the river goddess Naga leaves the gods for the mortal world and falls in love with a mortal, her defiance, and the gods' jealousy all lead to a devastating choice.

This book is a standalone prequel set in the world of *The River's Daughter*.

Published by Rising Grains Publishing

ISBN (eBook): 979-8-9987469-4-9

ISBN (Paperback): 979-8-9987469-5-6

Map illustration by Sarah Khan Azamy.

JARAAN
RUINS
TEMPLE OF JARAAN
MOUTH OF THE SERPENT
MARKET SQUARE
ELDER NEFRET'S HOUSE
WAYSTATION
GOVERNMENT COLONY
RIVER BARKI
MEHR'AN CAMP

IN THE FIRST AGE

In the First Age, Naga was water.

She raced and played with the other godlings, whom she called her brothers and her sisters, through darkness, and through the formation of spinning wheels of fire—exploring and dancing and destroying—until the Great Goddess made a singular world for them and bid them rule together.

Aag became god of fire. Havaa became goddess of wind, Zamīn goddess of earth, Raat and Din the twin gods of night and day. And Naga became the goddess of water.

Over the next ages, the Great Goddess filled their world with mortals.

And so the gods left behind the realm of stars where they first drew breath, and where the Great Goddess lived, and instead built new palaces for themselves closer to the mortals. Aag built himself a fire-mountain fortress at its center. Zamīn carved tunnels and caves into cliffs and into the ground far below. Havaa created wind-temples that moved where she wanted. The twins made their floating palaces in the sky:

places where they could play games, and watch the mortals below.

Only Naga needed no new, specific place to call her own; water went everywhere, and flowed through everything. She belonged to every place and to no place.

From their new watching places, for millennia, the gods ruled the world together.

Until Naga decided to leave.

PART ONE
GODS

CHAPTER 1
WAGERS

In the early years, when nothing in the mortal world yet had a name, the gods delighted themselves with building, and with destroying.

Aag's fires would burn settlements, making mortals run in search of water that Naga would then send to them in the form of torrential rain or waves that swept away towns. Zamīn's earthquakes sent the mortals grasping for trees that Havaa would then set spinning through the air. Raat would fill the mortals' minds with terrible images that jolted them out of peaceful rest, and Din worked with Aag to dry crops, and stop Naga's rains, and leave the mortals longing to quench their thirst.

But the Great Goddess had scolded them.

I made these mortals in your image. They should not be wasted so recklessly, she had said.

It was Zamīn who pointed out the obvious: Their lives were so short to begin with; their impermanence made their destruction immaterial—like a mortal stepping on an ant.

But the Great Goddess admonished her.

To them their lives are as long as their minds can hold. It is not for us to make them suffer for our amusement. You'll learn.

And they did.

Killing mortals was enjoyable, yes, but the gods learned to amuse themselves in gentler ways.

Havaa began to spread seeds for crops. But those most blessed by abundant harvests sometimes felt the wind pulling at them, and grew restless with wanderlust.

Aag learned to give warmth without burning—but the mortals who prayed to him sometimes found themselves filled with fury they couldn't name the source of.

Naga formed streams and created rainfall. But mortals who drank most deeply from her waters would sometimes feel a longing for something that was always just out of reach.

IN THESE EARLY YEARS, before the mortals started building their cities and making their kings, Naga and Aag would play a game:

Naga would form a raincloud, and make it hover over his fire-mountain. Aag would send his heat to dry it to the earth, before it could burst open.

Naga would form another one, and again, he would burn it away.

They played this game for centuries without tiring of it.

ONE DAY, Naga came to Aag's fortress. He was lying flat on his back, watching a bird circling high overhead.

"You'll set that bird ablaze," she warned.

"I made that bird," he answered, his eyes still tracking its movement.

She lay down beside him.

She turned slowly to look at him, and watched him a long while. "Your face is doing… something," she said finally.

"Hmm," he said.

"Hmm," she agreed. "Something is on your mind."

He sighed. "So it is." He turned slightly to look at her, but then looked back up at the bird again. "Ever since Ma ruined our fun—"

"What by asking us not to kill mortals indiscriminately?" Naga laughed. "Is that so bad?"

"If I abided by her wishes, it might be."

"Aag," Naga clucked.

"I'm only joking," he said, rolling his eyes.

Naga wasn't convinced.

He took a breath. "I've wondered if we should play some new games. Maybe even build a new world."

"Do you mean to suggest we leave this one?" She propped up onto her elbow. "You're bored. You need a change of scenery. Why not go the surface? Walk among them a while?"

Aag turned again to look at her. "Walk among the mortals?"

Naga shrugged.

"Why should a god want to walk among mortals?"

The light in his golden eyes was not unlike the sun's light, though his expression was unreadable. "No…" he said slowly. "I prefer to watch from my mountain."

Naga lay her head down now on her arm, saying nothing.

The heat radiating from him made her skin prickle.

She didn't move. She waited for the feeling to pass.

It always passed.

Aag stretched out his arms before clasping his hands behind his head. "Lately… you seem more interested in the mortal world than in our world."

"Their world is so fleeting, and yet they care so deeply about everything." She shook her head. "It's fascinating."

"They're mortals," he laughed. "They're *nothing*."

"Mortals are ephemeral," she conceded. "But they're not nothing."

Aag shook his head, his face growing serious.

Her face grew serious then too. "They're *not* nothing," she repeated. A pause. "I think I should like to see what it is to be among mortals."

"You'd wish to be with them?" Aag asked slowly. "Actually?"

She shrugged.

"You'd be far. From me."

Naga did not answer.

"I don't want you to be far."

The words hung heavy between them.

And then very gently, Naga spoke again. "Maybe some distance would do us some good."

Something in Aag's expression shifted then. Like he had put up a wall between them. And then he turned away, his eyes fixed on the bird again.

A long silence passed.

Eventually, Naga sat up, and moved away from the god of fire.

Just before she left, she turned and said lightly, "I'll send a raincloud to you again in the morning. Be ready."

There was a pause.

"I'll dry it," he said.

And once she was gone, he set the bird ablaze.

But Naga did not send a raincloud the next day.

Or the next year.

She did not return to his fortress for hundreds, and hundreds of years after that conversation.

I don't want you to be far, he had said.

And it changed things.

She had known, even when they were godlings, that he would want her to become something to him that she could not be.

She had known long ago that one day he would ask her for something that she would not want to give.

Had known from the day she first spoke that word:

Bhai.

As if the name could make it so.

She understood, eventually, what her walking away—her staying away for so long—would tell him.

Understood that he would not forgive her this.

But she could not belong to fire.

After a very, very long time, Naga called for all of her siblings to gather.

They agreed to meet at the edge of Aag's fire-mountain fortress.

When Naga arrived, Aag was sitting at the cliff's edge, watching the mortals below building a city, with channels of water that ran below ground.

"It is hard not to be impressed with what they've created, with such little time in each life," she observed in lieu of greeting.

"They are insignificant," Aag responded. And then a pause. "It's been nearly a thousand years."

"Come now," Naga said lightly. "Time is nothing to us, Bhai."

"*Bhai*," he repeated softly, turning the word over.

Naga turned her head and saw Havaa approaching.

She smiled as she approached, and her very presence made Naga feel more at ease.

Then Zamīn appeared from the earth, smoothing her robes—Raat trailing behind her, looking pleased with himself. He usually was only ever seen with his twin, Din—but he and Zamīn arrived together often enough… from deep in Zamīn's caves. Where no one watched.

"Bhai," Zamīn said, nodding to Aag, then touched Naga and Havaa's arms in greeting.

"Funny, I never hear you call Raat '*Bhai*,'" Din said approaching.

Zamīn ignored this and nodded instead at Naga. "Why have you called us to gather?"

Naga cleared her throat and stood. "I've decided to go spend some years living among the mortals." She paused. "As one of them. To see what it's like."

A long silence passed between the gods.

Zamīn spoke first. "It could be wise to experience the world from the perspective of the creatures upon it," she mused. Din and Raat snickered, but Zamīn ignored them. "There is precedent for it," she continued. "In other mortal worlds. In Ma's other realms… even some where gods walk among mortals."

"Enough," Aag said quietly.

Havaa shifted uncomfortably.

"But *why*?" Raat and Din asked in unison before laughing.

"I've been looking for…" Naga paused. "A change."

"An entire world to shape, and the water goddess finds complaint," Aag muttered.

"I don't find complaint," Naga said.

Aag smiled tightly. "Boredom, then?"

Naga sighed. "I only want to see what it's like to live as one of them."

"Or perhaps you're running from something here," Aag ventured.

"I'm not running from anything."

Din interrupted with a laugh. "Restricting yourself to the mortal world... What a waste of time."

"I'd lose interest within moments," Raat added laughing.

"Some say only the boring grow bored," Zamīn said coolly, and the smile quickly left Raat's face.

"Even a thousand years would be nothing," said Naga softly.

"Nothing?" Aag repeated, finding her eyes.

Naga met his gaze.

"Shall we wager, Naga?" Aag asked softly.

Zamīn cleared her throat. "Wagers by gods carry a great deal of weight and—"

"It is noted," Aag interrupted, his eyes fixed on Naga. "So, a wager?"

Naga ignored Zamīn's sounds of disapproving. "Name your terms."

"If you return before a thousand years, you must destroy the world and all its mortals with a great flood."

Havaa gasped. "But Ma said—"

Aag held up a hand, and continued addressing Naga alone. "But if you last the full thousand years, I'll..." A slow smile spread across his face. "I'll stop burning Havaa's villages."

"You've been doing *what*?" Havaa hissed.

"Yes. You'll stop," Naga interrupted, without looking at Havaa. "And during the course of the wager, you'll stop as well."

"Done," Aag said, extending a hand.

And before anyone else could say anything more, Naga slipped her own into his. "Done," she said. "I'll live with the mortals for a thousand years."

And the vow wove itself into the fabric of the mortal world, and into the very balance of all the gods' powers, binding them to the words they spoke.

Aag's eyes fixed on hers, and his voice dropped low. "A thousand years is a long time to prove a point, *Behen*."

"You're afraid I'll win."

He shook his head. "The mortals are beneath us," he said quietly. "You shame yourself."

"Bhai," she said softly.

"Don't." And then he turned.

The ground trembled as he walked away.

"Oh, Aag's jealous," Din sang after him. Then he turned to his twin and the two burst into laughter.

Havaa shook her head at the twins, and turned her attention back to Naga. "I can't believe he's been burning my villages. Even after Ma…" she trailed off.

"It is possible that he was… joking," Zamīn frowned, still watching Aag's retreating form. "He does fear losing control."

The twins were laughing again about something, and Naga shook her head.

She reached forward to squeeze Havaa's hand. "Even if it's true, he won't do it again. Not during this wager, and not after I win."

Havaa smiled gratefully at her.

Zamīn watched Naga thoughtfully. "Enjoy your time," she said.

Naga nodded gratefully.

And soon after, the goddess of wind, and of earth, and the twin gods of night and day left Naga alone.

Tomorrow, Naga would go and live among the mortals.

For a thousand years.

CHAPTER 2
MORTALS

Naga had been right.

Even a thousand years would be nothing.

When she came to the earth, Naga created a body for herself. It was an average of many mortal bodies she had seen and found pleasing to look at; medium in stature, mostly female in sex, dark in skin. The body's strong legs let her climb hills and jump onto tall rocks. The arms let her grasp at branches and pull herself up into trees.

She relished the feeling of Zamīn's mud squishing between her toes when she walked slowly through forest floor. When she moved more quickly, she felt Havaa's wind rustling the hairs on her arms and legs, and relished that, too. The sensation was so pleasing that she became obsessed with it, and with running.

She spent months running, stopping only to drink water, or catch flying creatures in her hands, or to sample fruits that hung from the trees.

Some years later, she decided to try staying still.

She spent days lying on the forest floor, watching bees flitting from flower to flower, butterflies fluttering their wings, spiders weaving sparkling crystalline patterns.

She spent weeks simply watching the trees.

And as she watched, new leaves began to sprout, and then unfurl. Small white flowers blossomed on vines that curled down, intending to touch her.

She let them.

She lay down on the bank, trailing her hands through the flowing currents of the rivers she herself had made, surrounded by flowers and green things.

It was intoxicating.

More years passed, and soon she longed to explore her waters. She decided to adjust her mortal form to be longer, leaner, more lithe—more able to move like a serpent, as easily through water as grass and forest.

She taught herself to breathe underwater.

She traveled along creeks she spun into streams, and then molded into rivers. She wove the rivers through forests, to jungles, and back again, swimming and weaving from place to place, creating new channels in places where the trees grew denser, and the smell of cold pine gave way to heat, and wet, green smells.

Weeks melted into months and years, and then decades went by and she scarcely noticed.

She learned, eventually, to sleep.

AFTER HUNDREDS of years of wandering, exploring, creating alone, and sleeping alone, she began to grow lonely.

And she began to visit the mortals.

At first she went to their villages under the cover of darkness, lingering only at the edges. Listening to their conversations. Learning their songs. Watching them playing with their children. Tending to their dying.

But eventually, she was tempted to go closer.

If there were enough people bustling through a market, she would cover her face in a cloak, and walk into the crowd, relishing the feel of all the mortal bodies pushing past one another.

She learned to want.

Sometimes, a beautiful young man would come close to the forest edge, and she'd remove her cloak, and draw the man into the darkness.

She learned quickly that mortal men were different from gods. They were rough in some ways, and yet softer too in their fragility—in their powerlessness. It delighted her.

But more than once after lying with a mortal man, she left feeling emptier than before, and she would leave that place to find a new one—a new place, with new people.

She moved often.

But no matter where she went, so much happened among mortals.

One century, there was a war.

She knew of war and loss and the killing of hundreds of thousands of mortals, of course. In the gods' games in the early years, she'd killed at least so many herself without a second thought.

But it was a different thing to walk through battlefields in a mortal body, seeing moonlight glinting off the mortals' sharp killing tools.

A different thing to walk amid the suffocating stink of rotting flesh, the smell of blood on the earth.

And even in the cold night air, she could feel, always, the lingering heat of flames she couldn't see.

Aag.

And night after night, she would hear fighting, and hours later, walk through fields of blood and metal and again, that lingering heat.

She did nothing to stop it.

ONE YEAR, Naga saw to a woman lying in the dirt, clutching her swollen stomach.

She had walked away from so many dead bodies during the war. She began to walk away now.

But something made her stop. Maybe the knowledge that this woman could be helped; that this woman wasn't dead yet.

And so she came near.

The woman lying in a pool of her own blood, crying and clutching at her womb, begging for help she could never have imagined would really come.

And Naga knelt down beside the woman and pressed her hands to the woman's belly. She felt something shift.

But then the woman clawed at Naga's hands. "You are either a god or a witch," the woman gasped, terror in her face. "I do not want you!"

"I am helping you," Naga had told her, trying to touch her stomach again, trying to help them both.

But the woman reached forward and scratched across Naga's face, screaming again for her to leave.

Naga roared in frustration.

She sat beside the woman in silence, watching her cry and scream and yet reject the only help that was available.

Finally, Naga walked away.

She stayed in the tree-line and watched the woman shake and cry and suffer.

CHAPTER 2

She watched the woman die.

Soon, the woman's child died too.

～

AFTER THAT, Naga became obsessed with women with swollen bellies—women like the one who hadn't let her save her or her child.

She went to a town where she could watch everything from the forest at its edge. She watched from the periphery as women in the town had children, and then, from a distance, Naga watched over the children. Years later, when those children grew up Naga watched the children's children, too.

She kept telling herself that these mortals, with their fleeting lives were beneath her.

Yet she could not stop watching.

She watched them live, and suffer, and love, and grieve, and die.

～

IT WAS NEARLY A CENTURY LATER, in another village, in another kingdom, that Naga saw another woman with swollen belly, lying in the dirt, begging for help she could never have imagined would come.

And something came over Naga and before she even knew what she was doing, she was on her knees before the woman, putting her hands on her womb.

This time, the dying woman with a swollen belly let her help. And Naga saved the woman and her child.

And something in Naga's heart began to stitch itself back together.

They were beneath her, she told herself again.

But then some years later, in another village, there was another woman.

And then another.

She told herself over and over again that they were beneath her. But years of women Naga had never meant to know, or to love, or to grieve later, she wasn't sure she believed it.

ONE CENTURY, there was an illness that made many, many children sick.

Naga went to each of them.

She placed her hands upon their faces.

But there was something in their illness that her power seemed not to be able to reach. Something in their blood that seemed to come from a place beyond the mortal realm, and there was nothing she could do.

The people of that village, who knew she had visited each child, and saw each child die, decided she was a witch.

That she caused the deaths of all of their children.

They decided she should die.

When she learned of this, something dark and cold moved through her. She could drown them all. She *should* drown them all.

Instead, she ran, and swore she would not repeat her mistake. The mortals were beneath her.

SHE RAN and ran and ran, deeper and deeper into a forest that seemed to have no end.

And deep in the heart of that forest, she tore a new river in the earth.

It flowed and danced and raged.

She made it her home.

SHE SPENT the next three centuries alone. Away from the mortals. Away from life, and from war, and from illness, and from death.

And from rejection.

She stopped thinking of the mortals and their short, fickle lives.

But she thought of her siblings now constantly.

Zamīn in soft grass underfoot, Havaa in the breeze, Din in sunlight, Raat in moonlight. Even Aag when she built fires against the cold, though those thoughts were complicated.

But she found she could not remember the sound of Havaa's laugh. Naga sat very still and tried harder to remember. But she couldn't.

Eventually she stopped trying.

SOME NINE HUNDRED and eighty years passed.

Nearly the thousand she'd promised Aag.

And then, it was year nine hundred and ninety.

And then, she met Rajan.

CHAPTER 3

PRINCES

It was a hot, sticky morning when Naga lay her body down by her river. Her fingers trailed through the rippling, dappled golden light on the water's surface. She closed her eyes, taking in the smell of jasmine, and rain, and earth, and river.

"Are you alright?"

Naga's fingers froze, and she rolled slowly onto her back.

A mortal man peered down at her, concern creasing his young, bronzed face.

"Madam? Are you alright?"

Naga didn't move for a moment, but then she carefully made her way to her feet. "Yes," she said, smoothing her long, wet robe. "I am alright."

She took in his appearance. He had shortly cropped dark hair and broad shoulders, and wore a long tunic. The weapon at his hip was a sword. He glanced back, checking for something. As he looked away, her eyes went to his hands. They were rougher than the hands of the mortal men she'd taken into the forest. But they were cleaner, too—no dirt underneath the fingernails.

He turned back and stepped closer, his eyes moving over her in turn. Her amber eyes. Her long, serpentine body… her wet robe.

He shook his head, as if clearing it. "Are you hurt?" he asked. When she shook her head, he looked confused. "Why are you out here by the river? Alone?"

"I'm fine," she said, looking up into his face.

And that's when she noticed his eyes. A brown so dark, and so deep, that they looked black.

He looked nothing like her brothers, with their glowing eyes and gold skin.

"But you're bleeding," he pointed out.

Naga looked down to see a long, slim gash on her leg. She must have scraped it on a rock or branch when she got up.

The man came closer still. "Let me help you," he said gently.

Naga cocked her head to the side. "How would you help me? You are a mortal."

The man raised his brows.

"As am I," she added then, quickly. "We are both mortal."

The man continued to look at her. "Yes, we are both mortals," he agreed, nodding slowly. He extended a hand. "Why don't you come forward? This river's water is pure. We can rinse that injury."

Naga nodded and allowed the man to guide her forward toward her river. She felt the rush of cool water lap against her foot.

For the briefest moment, she became aware of the sting of the cut, and felt the urge to change her form—to reset the injury.

She resisted the urge. She instead allowed herself to feel the sensations: the pain, the coolness of the water, the feel of the calluses of his hands on her skin.

He finished cleaning the injury to his satisfaction, and then motioned for her to return to the bank.

She sat down on a large rock and watched him tear a strip of cloth from the bottom of his tunic, and wring it dry.

"May I?" he asked. She nodded. She watched as he knelt at her feet, bandaging her leg carefully.

"You're not… from around here," the man said finally, settling back down beside her.

"Why do you say this?" she asked.

"You…" he paused. "To start with, you're out here alone. And," he cleared his throat, "you seem not to know who I am."

Naga tilted her head. "Who are you?"

The man laughed.

Naga reached forward and grasped his face.

He froze under the unexpected aggression, but did not make any attempt to remove her hand. Behind him, an animal shifted and snorted in the trees. The man's eyes darted to the side briefly, but he did not move.

"Is that a friend of yours?"

"It is my horse, Bakki."

"I am Naga," she said. "Not Bakki."

"No, I meant… no, my horse is named Bakki."

"Alright. And who are you?"

His eyes narrowed slightly. "I am Rajan."

She stared at him.

"You've never heard the name?" His brows furrowed. "Rajan of the house of Jaraan? I am the youngest son of Rajni of Jaraan, Queen of this land."

She finally released his face. "Son of a Queen." She frowned. "A future king, then?"

He rubbed his jaw, and kept his eyes fixed on hers. "No… just a younger brother to a future king. A prince."

She pondered this.

Second to the future king. And he had named himself by his mother—not by his father's name, and not by his title.

"That name—Rajni of Jaraan—it doesn't mean anything to you," he realized.

There was a long silence between them.

"Well. If what you claim is true, you are still the son of a ruler, Rajan of Jaraan," she said finally, a warmth growing inside her.

"Prince Ra—" he began, before changing course. "Yes."

She nodded, a decision made.

"Good. I, too, am the daughter of a ruler."

Rajan's brows rose. "How's that?"

"I am the daughter of the Great Goddess. I am the goddess of water."

Rajan nodded slowly, realizing now that the woman before him was completely crazy.

He began to clear his throat, intending to announce that he would take his leave, when she spoke again.

"I have an idea, Rajan of Jaraan," she said, a slow smile spreading across her face. "I think I would like to have you."

"Have me?" His voice caught. "What are you talking about?"

In answer, she opened her robe and let it drop down over her shoulders.

Before he could take in this new turn of events, something caught his eye, and his attention went to her bandaged leg.

"A snake! On your—madam, you have a snake on your leg!"

Naga tilted her head to the side.

"A snake!" Rajan said more insistently. "Do not worry, I will aid you," he said—but he swallowed as he inched closer.

"A snake is a friend," Naga said, smiling. And then she reached down.

Moments later, she stood, and the snake's long winding form had wrapped itself around her arm.

"He won't hurt me," she cooed, "or you."

Rajan of Jaraan seemed to be fighting the urge to scream as Naga, her arm now fully wrapped by the snake—its iridescent scales shimmering in the thin beam of light that streamed in through the tree cover—stepped closer to him.

He stumbled back, but she reached down and grabbed him by his tunic. She pulled at the neck, her strength far exceeding what her body seemed that it should be able to do, and lifted him up from the ground, pulling him close.

He gasped at her strength, and then swallowed, trying to regain his composure. It was difficult. "How are you doing this?"

Naga laughed then, a deep, hearty laugh.

"It's a special power," she whispered, the snake curling further down her arm, moving closer to Rajan's tunic, its mouth making its way toward his neck.

"I don't understand..." Rajan whispered. "Who are you?"

She let him go then, and he nearly fell to the ground. She caressed the snake on her arm before slowly letting it unwind itself and return to the forest floor. "I'm a goddess. I've already told you."

"Right." His face twisted in concentration. "But where are you from? If you're a commoner then–"

Naga laughed heartily then. "A commoner?"

"An outsider then?" He offered. "I... I'm sorry. I don't know what you are. I'm only trying to understand what's—" He paused. "Where do you *live*? What *are* you?"

The snake had slithered over to Rajan's foot and was slowly making its way up his leg.

Just as he looked down, Naga laughed again, and this time, she opened her mouth wide.

As she did, she allowed her jaw to unhinge itself, her mouth opening wider and wider.

And wider.

Rajan gasped and drew back in horror, stumbling, unsure whether to fight off the snake, or run from the nightmare unfolding before him.

But the snake was wrapped around both legs now, and he fell backward, landing hard on the ground. It tightened around his ankles, locking him in place.

And his eyes fixed helplessly on Naga's opening mouth.

And suddenly…

He could see, and hear, and feel, the entire ocean.

Inside her mouth.

The sound of waves crashing on shores, the rising of tides, the sensation of being rocked on the sea. All of it suddenly felt visceral and real to him in a way he couldn't explain. And as he looked inside her mouth, he saw eternity in liquid form.

Endless oceans, rivers that carved continents, rains that had fallen since time began.

And then suddenly, her mouth snapped shut and the real world set back in.

The snake that had bound his legs was nowhere to be seen. Naga's mouth was just an ordinary mouth.

"I am no outsider, nor commoner. I am Naga. I am the goddess of the water."

Rajan began to breathe hard and fast.

His eyes darted from her mouth to her eyes and he struggled to find words, gasping for air that wouldn't come.

"Breathe, Rajan of Jaraan," she whispered, and then without any effort he could measure, his breathing slowed.

He steadied himself, lifting himself from the ground, one

hand bracing against a tree. He looked at her again, and stood up straighter. "If you're a goddess, why were you... just... lying in the mud, alone?"

The question surprised her. "Because I choose to be alone," she said softly.

"It doesn't make sense." He squared his shoulders, but she saw that his hands still trembled. "It seems like a waste."

Naga turned her head to the side, gazing at this fragile, scared thing, standing so bravely before her.

She could drown him in her rivers so easily.

Instead, she moved closer to him.

"Rajan of Jaraan, you speak very boldly to one so much more powerful than you," she said, and blue marks began to blossom on her skin, coiling around her arms like horrible snakes.

She reached forward and held his jaw as she had done earlier.

Rajan swallowed, and met her eyes.

The forest seemed to go quiet.

There was only the singing of the river, and the smell of earth and wet and green and jasmine now. Even the air between them was still.

"Let me show you what gods are like," she said.

His mouth opened, but no sound emerged.

And then, she untied her robe and let it drop to the wet ground.

The air cooled her bare skin.

He swallowed.

And then, beneath the trees, Naga made Rajan hers.

CHAPTER 4
LOVERS

After, Naga had meant to leave.

He was just a mortal.

But then the night had fallen while their bodies were still entangled, and then dawn had too, and she had woken beside the prince.

"Stay," he murmured as she drew out of his embrace.

"I won't do that," she said, kneeling as she slipped on her robe and fastened it closed.

He propped himself up on his elbow. "Where are you going?"

"Into the river," she said, stretching her arms. She stood and began to leave. "Goodbye, Rajan of Jaraan."

"Wait!" he called, brushing off his legs and scrambling up to follow her. "What do you mean, 'into the river?'"

She moved gracefully over gnarled roots and under branches. "I mean I'm going to become a water serpent and swim into the bottom of the river," she said, as if describing what she'd eat for lunch.

"Slow down," he called, stumbling over a felled log. "How will I find you again?"

She stopped abruptly, and he had to brace himself from running into her. She turned and looked at him thoughtfully. "You *were* very attentive last night," she said slowly, ignoring the blush creeping into his face.

She reached down and picked up a small, blueish stone. She ran a finger over it, and a jagged spiral pattern appeared, etched into its surface. "Take this, Rajan of Jaraan," she said, placing it in the mortal prince's hand. "And you can find your way back to me."

He stared at the stone in his hand.

When he looked back up, she was gone, and there were only ripples on the surface of the river.

RAJAN OF JARAAN had heard the story of the river goddess since he was old enough to hear stories, of course.

When his father was alive, he had told him of a goddess who walked among mortals, healed the sick, and fed the crops with her tears.

His older brother Adhiraj told him a different version, in which the river goddess ate snakes, killed men, and drowned cities.

Adhiraj's wife, Maya Bhabi, told Rajan that the river goddess kept the world alive.

Rajan's own mother had once told him the river goddess was just a story told to boys as a euphemism for ladies who walked the riverbank in search of men to seduce. She had told him to be wary of walking the river alone.

Rajan returned to the river the next morning.

And the morning after that, and the one after that one.

ONE MORNING, the mortal prince asked her about what she'd once shown him, in her mouth.

"Will you let me see it again?" he asked, remembering the feeling of being on waves.

"I regret showing you," she confessed. "It is much too much for your mortal mind. I fear it has changed you."

"I demand it."

She raised an eyebrow but said nothing.

"I—" he started. "I request it."

"And why," she said slowly, "should I grant what you request?"

"Because I am your prince," he said carefully.

"I am a goddess of the entire mortal realm. Your title means nothing to me."

He straightened his back. "Because I am your lover."

"Lover!" She clapped her hands in delight. "How deliciously mortal of you. My *lover*," she cooed.

"I—" he began. "Please," he whispered, lowering himself to his knees. "Please."

"Please, what?"

"Please, show me what you showed me. That first day. When you opened your mouth wide. Please. I can't stop thinking about it."

And then she moved closer to him.

And obliged.

Moments later, his hands and knees were on the ground and he was gasping.

She reached down to stroke his cheek, and he sat back onto his knees, looking up through tears into her eyes.

The vastness should have destroyed his mind, he knew. It should have shattered his very sense of reality.

But what he felt instead was a desperate yearning for more of her. "Thank you," he whispered, pressing his cheek into her hand, like a child taking comfort in his mother.

"A devotee in the making," Naga murmured down at him, her thumb gently stroking his face.

"I could be devoted to you," he whispered, gazing up at her through unfocused eyes. "I could worship you."

This goddess who could show him the entire ocean.

ONE DAY RAJAN brought her a carved wooden serpent. "For you," he said, turning the carving over. "Because you are unafraid."

Naga smiled and reached forward to take the serpent from his hands. Rajan's eyes were fixed on her hands as she traced the carved coils with her finger. "I am unafraid because I am like a serpent. Fluid. Always in motion." Blue swirled lightly along her forearms before disappearing. She looked up at him. "What are you in your true form, Rajan?"

He swallowed. "I don't know."

But then he laughed, suddenly remembering himself, remembering he was a prince, and smoothed his tunic.

She watched him with amusement.

A mortal, with so little time to understand himself.

And yet…

She felt something that she couldn't name. It wasn't that he was… anything more than a mortal. But he was… just a mortal.

She knew she was paying close attention to his voice, to his responses, to the way he swallowed when he didn't have an answer…

He was memorable, that was all. He was singular, even.

Even, maybe, irreplaceable.

She looked away, and watched the river instead.

The river made sense.

AND THEN THERE were seven mornings he did not come.

She pretended she wasn't counting them.

She was counting them.

On the seventh day, she made it rain in the kingdom.

It wasn't to call him to her; it was just a coincidental desire she had to make it rain in the kingdom. The land in the kingdom just looked thirsty. But why wasn't he coming to her anyway? Not that she cared that he wasn't coming. But where was he?

When he finally came, he looked unlike himself.

He looked disturbed. Distraught.

He did not speak to her, but sat alone at the bank of the river, pulling on long pieces of grass.

She observed him for a long while before she spoke.

"What troubles you, Rajan of Jaraan?"

He was quiet for a long time before he spoke. "My mother is dying." He glanced at her. "Which… it is fine. She isn't in pain." He swallowed.

Naga nodded. "I am sorry."

He took a deep breath. "And she has abdicated already. She has named Adhiraj King." He shook his head slowly. "I've always known it was coming, of course, but…"

"She has ruled alone, your mother?"

Rajan laughed bitterly. "You mean without my father? Yes. He has been long dead. Slain by my mother's council, in fact."

Naga's eyes widened.

"Offended?" Rajan asked wryly.

"Impressed, actually." She frowned. "And you cannot have two kings?"

He looked at her, incredulous. "Two kings?"

"We have many gods," she shrugged.

He watched her thoughtfully, before shaking his head. "No. No, we can't—" he stopped, on the precipice of something. "No. She doesn't believe in shared power, and my brother..." he cleared his throat. "No, he's the rightful king. His wife Maya is the daughter of the House of Daraio. Even their house is one of great power."

"Do I not have power?" Naga smiled.

"A different sort of power." He smiled ruefully. "And anyway, I'm just the younger brother. He was always meant to rule."

"And what were you meant to do?"

"Support Adhiraj. Or I can refuse."

"And if you don't serve him? If you simply... walk away?"

Rajan's eyes were far away for a moment. "Then I'd be abandoning the people I was raised to protect. My mother didn't choose me to rule, but she raised me to serve. If I leave, Adhiraj rules alone, and he..."

Naga waited.

"He doesn't feel things the way I do." Rajan laughed, but it was not a happy sound. "'A ruler who feels too much cannot do what ruling requires,'" he recited. Then he sighed. "He sees the kingdom as a machine. I see it as people."

"I wouldn't want to serve my brother either," Naga said quietly.

"I never said—" Rajan broke off, and then shook his head. "It's not that I don't want to serve him. It's... complicated."

Naga nodded. Waited.

"I do want to serve the people. And I've been given

education. I've been trained to be Adhiraj's second since I was born. It's my job to serve. To reject that role would be…" he trailed off.

"And so?" Naga prompted. "If you reject the role, if you walk away… so?"

He looked at her, perplexed. "So, I'd be rejecting my duty."

Naga narrowed her eyes. "And duty is the most important thing to you?"

"I…" he paused. "I don't know what the most important thing is to me now."

Naga was quiet a long time. She watched the water of her river. It swirled and twisted and danced. She thought of snakes then. Of shedding skin.

"When snakes shed their skin, they don't die," she said, her eyes still on the water. "They can shed their skin, again and again. Becoming something new."

"I'm no snake," he said quietly.

"It's true for everyone," she said, moving closer to him. "You can shed your skin too."

He shook his head.

"Don't you know, Rajan of Jaraan," she continued, moving even closer. "That you can do anything you want?"

He laughed bitterly. "Yes, I'm sure that's true for gods and goddesses."

"It's true for everyone," she murmured, climbing onto his lap, her arms sliding around his neck.

He looked up into her eyes with surprise.

"You can shed everything. You can shed the prince you're supposed to be, and become something new." And she dropped her lips to his neck, and pushed him down into the grass.

And then there was no more talking between them.

"WHAT IS it like to be you?" he asked one day.

"You truly wish to know?"

He nodded.

She motioned for him to close his eyes, and then sat beside him, guiding his hands into the water. "Do you feel how the water moves around your hands?"

"I feel it."

"No, you're feeling the water against you. Feel how it moves around you."

"What's the difference?"

"The water flows around your hands. It forms itself around you. Around the shape of you."

She moved closer and put her hands into the water near his. "That's what it is to be me. It is like this with everything for me. Every stone, every kingdom, every person I have ever met..." she moved her hands around his, circling them. "I have flowed around them. Taken in the shape of them. I will carry the shape of them inside of me forever."

He looked up from the water and met her eyes. "That's a long time to carry something."

"It has always been this way. Since all my time on earth. Since the beginning of time, really. Everything I've ever seen. Every person I've..." she paused. "I carry everything I've ever experienced."

He took her hands in his then, under the water.

She straightened her spine. "But I am also the current. I can pull you into my depths." Her eyes flashed. "I can destroy. And you'd be powerless to stop me." And then she let her power course into his skin, for just a moment, making him gasp.

He looked at her, panting, eyes wide.

"Do you regret asking?"

He was still panting, but then he slowed his breathing.

And then slowly, deliberately, he met her gaze. "No."

And this time he was the one who reached for her and pulled her into his embrace.

$$\sim$$

ONE DAY, some seasons later, Rajan came to her with a look she had never seen in his face before.

"Run away with me," he had said. "And we can be together."

Her brows lifted. "We're together now."

He inhaled. "If I stay, I can't take you as my bride, because…"

"Because I'm a god," she finished for him.

He stared at her. "Because you're… a commoner."

She laughed.

He shook his head. "And—I don't care. But the court will. Adhiraj will."

She reached forward and touched his face. "And so?" she asked.

"And so we have to go," he pleaded.

"And if I say I want to stay here?" Naga smiled, and then cupped his jaw, tilting his chin so his gaze was fixed on hers.

"Then…" he felt his body respond to her, to her proximity, to her intensity. "Then I'd kill my brother if you asked. Make you my queen."

He froze, as if only now realizing what he'd said.

"I—" his eyes were wide.

But she only laughed with delight. "Your queen? What would I want with being a queen?"

But he reached up to catch her wrist, where her hand still

held his face, his eyes still full of worry. "Why did I say that?" he whispered.

She searched his eyes—and there it was.

Devotion.

He was no longer a devotee in the making. His eyes held the kind of devotion that had started wars, drowned cities, reshaped the world.

He had meant it, and that was what was scaring him.

"Offering to make me a queen," she said, shaking her head. "When I'm already a goddess."

She let his face go then, but he didn't immediately release her wrist.

He swallowed. "Why wouldn't you want... I mean if I *had* meant it, why wouldn't you—"

She gazed at him. "Why would *you* offer it to me?"

"Because... I... I think I've become obsessed with you," he whispered. "I fear there is nothing I wouldn't do for you. It's as if... there are no stars in the sky. Nothing else. There's only you."

She nodded slowly, approvingly. "Good."

One morning, Naga found Rajan sitting beside the river on a large flat rock, washing blood from a wound on his arm.

He winced as she approached. "I'm fine," he assured her before she came close.

"You are hurt," she observed. She knelt beside him and placed her hand over the wound. Water flowed from her palm, washing away blood and pain.

When she stepped back his skin was healed. Perfect.

Rajan looked down at the place there had been a gash and

shook his head. "Someday," he said, "you won't be able to fix me."

She looked at him strangely, and stood up, turning away from him. "Mortals live many years, Rajan of Jaraan."

"Not that many," he said slowly, and reached for her hand. "And you'll still go on. Forever. Even after I'm gone. Right?"

"That is right," she said slowly. She let him pull her closer.

"And when I'm gone, I'll have been but a moment in your long life," he said softly.

She said nothing.

"But for me, there's... nothing else." He swallowed. "I want to give you... my entire life."

Some new, unfamiliar feeling tightened in Naga's chest.

She wrapped her arms around his neck, ignoring it. "Your entire life isn't *so* long, Rajan of Jaraan," she brushed her lips tenderly against his warm face.

"Then—then it should be nothing to you," he said, clearing his throat. "Staying with me for my mortal life. For all of it."

She watched him carefully, taking in his question.

What it meant to him to ask this.

And then, she momentarily froze as a second thought occurred to her: What it would mean for her—*to* her—when he was gone.

Something stung her eyes.

She quickly blinked it away.

"Let me... let me belong to you," he whispered.

Her throat tightened. "You already do," she said lightly.

"Then give me your word. You... won't be my wife, but... You'll be... you'll stay. Until the end of my life."

She looked at Rajan for a long moment.

Looked into his eyes that were so deep and dark that they looked black.

Saw the devotion looking back at her.

And the feeling in her throat became a pain.

And in that moment, she knew that after he was gone, she would carry him inside of her for the rest of time.

She knew that however long his life was, it was never going to be enough.

That the weight of him, and of his devotion, and of one day losing him would never lessen.

"I swear it," she said finally. "Until the end of your life."

RAINCLOUDS

Naga was sitting beside the river with the mortal, her head thrown back, laughing about something.

She laughed the same way she had laughed when she was young, and nothing on the mortal world had yet been named.

Aag sat in his fire-mountain watching. He could have reached down to the riverbank to listen to what the mortal had said that she found so funny.

But he did not want to know.

He had been watching Naga off and on for centuries. Watched her slipping past mortals as she delighted from afar in their festivals, and he had felt nothing. Watched her soothe a child whose mother died, before she pulled up her cloak and retreated into a forest, and he had felt nothing.

Watched her walk through a war she didn't stop, stepping around the dead—pausing at the heat that inexplicably radiated from the bodies of the dead.

And he had felt nothing.

He only watched out of curiosity. He had been waiting for her to finish her thousand years. To finish the wager, and be done with the realm of mortals. He had been waiting for her to come back.

He watched her lean into the mortal and caress his face.

And then Aag's mountain shuddered.

Absently, he felt aware of the attention of his other siblings over the distances. Felt Zamīn reaching her attention over the earth, checking for his mood. He felt her receding, leaving him to his solitude.

Felt Havaa's air go still.

Below, Naga hadn't moved. Hadn't reacted, hadn't shifted, hadn't made any movement to show she felt the tremor of Aag's mountain.

Long ago, she would have. When they were godlings, she would have.

He steadied himself. It was better this way. Fire and water only destroyed one another.

It was better she amuse herself with a mortal.

He didn't care.

He took another deep breath, pulling his heat inward.

Stillness. Stillness would have to be his peace.

And then he saw the mortal removing the clothing that covered Naga's mortal form.

And Aag stopped watching them.

Far, far, far below Aag's fire-mountain, something was breaking.

Zamīn had made the earth's surface, and Havaa had filled it with breath, and the twins had made the mortals learn to count hours, but there, in the deepest fiery belly of the mortals' world, was Aag's heart.

It was breaking.

Had it ever broken before?

Absently, he remembered their game. When Naga would form a raincloud, and make it hover over his fire-mountain, and he would send his heat to dry it to the earth.

And without fully thinking about what he was doing, he began to dry Naga's rivers.

It was no different than drying her rainclouds, he told himself.

The vow he had sworn in their wager quivered under the weight of his choice.

It was no different than drying her rainclouds, he told himself again.

Across the distance, Aag knew his brothers Din and Raat would not interfere. He knew Zamīn would sense what he was doing, but she would not stop him. Havaa, he knew, would feel it too, and would say nothing.

He began to let the rains slow.

It was no different than drying her rainclouds.

And he began to reach down slowly, through the distance, pulling the moisture from the world. From every river, from every ocean.

It was no different than drying her rainclouds.

And he began to press his heat, heavy and dry, down onto the mortal world.

DROUGHT

The rains had begun to slow.

Naga woke one morning to find her body changed in ways she hadn't anticipated. Her skin felt different. It itched in some places. Her mouth felt dry. Her breasts felt tender.

And something was missing.

That thrum of power that was always there just under her skin. She couldn't find it.

She walked to her river, and felt herself straining as she reached for her powers.

When she arrived, she found the water sitting lower than it ever before had.

And it seemed to be dropping lower as she watched.

She shook her head and tried to summon a light rain.

A thin trickle of moisture beaded on her palms but, from the skies... Nothing.

She swallowed.

For the first time since taking mortal form, she felt fear.

Rajan arrived moments later, and seemed to freeze as he

took in the river. And then, he turned, and saw Naga staring at her hands.

"What's wrong?"

"I can't seem to…" She tried again, and tiny raindrop landed on her nose. "My powers. They aren't…"

Another solitary raindrop fell. What could be causing this?

And then her eyes grew wide. What if…

Rajan looked at her, patiently waiting for an explanation. She swallowed.

"I'm carrying your child."

THE WORDS HUNG BETWEEN THEM.

She had never carried mortal life inside a mortal body. She did not know its cost. She could not have known.

Rajan's eyes widened.

But then a smile spread over his face, filling it with joy she had never seen before. "A child."

"A half-mortal child," Naga said carefully, watching for his reaction.

He knelt beside her, placing his hands in hers. "Our child."

Her eyes fixed on his. "My siblings will see this as… unacceptable."

"A child," Rajan said, his eyes alight with wonder. And then he wrapped his arms around her and spun her around, and she couldn't help but laugh too.

And for just a moment, she stopped thinking about the power she could not feel surging beneath her skin.

AFTER RAJAN LEFT, he remained absent for many days.

The first morning he didn't come, Naga reminded herself that such things had happened before, that he'd return soon —that he did have a job as a prince.

The next morning he didn't come, Naga spent the entire day trying to force her power to surge through her hands, to feel for it in her blood, with no luck.

By the third morning, she felt herself growing briefly irritated. But she brushed away the feeling, throwing herself into trying to force her powers to surge forth from her fingertips. She thought she felt a brief spark of something, but it was gone as quickly as it had come.

On the fourth morning, she went to the side of her river and frowned, trying to determine if it looked even lower than before. And then she remembered the look of joy in Rajan's face as he spun her around. *A child.*

The fifth morning, Naga was growing worried about Rajan. And then she came to her river to find the water was even lower.

And then a chill.

What if the power she couldn't feel in her body was also absent from the mortal world itself?

What if her baby was the cause of—

She pushed the thought away.

She tried again to summon it. The thrumming she hadn't felt under her skin in days. It wouldn't come.

The sixth morning, the river was so low that there were some places she could see its bed.

And it hadn't rained again.

ON THE SEVENTH MORNING, Rajan returned.

And Naga barely recognized him. His face was gaunt, his eyes hollow.

"Tell me," she said quietly.

"My mother has died," he said, his voice flat, stepping into her embrace.

Naga held him, but he did not fall into her embrace weeping. Instead, he continued in a flat voice. "Something is wrong. There are children in the kingdom. They're... I think they're dying."

Naga stepped back and looked at his face in confusion. "The children?"

"The drought. Something isn't right. All the water in the wells, the stores... drying up." He shrugged helplessly. "I spoke to a man this morning. He told me they haven't had any water in their barrels in days. The well near their home is already empty. They're giving their children squeezed fruit juice but..." He shook his head. "Something isn't right," he said again.

Naga's hands shook. A very human thing, she knew.

"I think it's me," she whispered.

Rajan looked at her.

"The drought. My... powers." She shook her head. "I think it's the—a half mortal child. It might be costing the world its water."

Rajan froze. "How... certain are you?"

Naga shook her head. "I don't know. But I can feel... something is missing. Something that should be here, under my skin, isn't."

Rajan stared at her for a long moment.

Then he swallowed and sat up straighter. "So it ends when the baby is here."

Naga said nothing.

"Months, then."

Naga still said nothing.

"We'll figure it out," Rajan said, his voice too bright.

RAJAN COULDN'T STAY. He told Naga he was needed in the palace. He had been summoned by his brother to deal with the drought and its fallout.

In his absence, Naga again tried to summon rain. She could not feel her power humming under the surface of her mortal skin or in her blood or in her fingers.

Still, she tried again.

And again.

And no matter what she did, how hard she forced the power to come from her hands, or her mind, nothing happened.

But hadn't she heard that the Great Goddess had carried half-mortals in her own womb?

Naga shook her head. But no. The Great Goddess was the Great Goddess. Naga was only water.

The sky remained cloudless.

"Why won't it work?" she demanded of the empty sky.

No answer came.

IT WAS Adhiraj's oldest advisor who greeted Rajan in the palace upon his arrival.

"Where have you been, sahib?"

"Pankaj," Rajan said in greeting, walking past the older man. "Where is my brother?"

"Occupied, sahib," he said, skipping to keep up with Rajan's pace. "Where were you?"

"The forest. Hunting."

"For five days, sahib?"

Rajan turned to look at him sharply and the advisor lowered his head in deference. "I meant no disrespect. But King Adhiraj—" Rajan winced, but Pankaj continued as if he didn't notice. "He asks me constantly—has been asking me for months actually—where you are and… I have no answer."

They were almost at the royal study now, and Rajan took a deep breath, reminding himself that Pankaj was only trying to do his duty. "I'll deal with my brother myself," he said, keeping his voice steady.

"As you think is best," Pankaj said, and nodded to the two guards outside the room to let him in.

Rajan stepped through the door to the royal study.

Adhiraj was sitting hunched over his desk. He looked up and for the briefest moment, his face brightened. Then his expression went flat again.

"Bhai," Adhiraj said, motioning to the chair in front of his desk.

"Anything for my king," Rajan said in greeting, bowing his body far lower than was needed.

"Get up." Adhiraj groaned.

Rajan obliged.

"Our mother built this kingdom and entrusted us to care for it," Adhiraj began.

"And so you do," Rajan said, sitting down in the chair opposite Adhiraj.

"Don't joke," Adhiraj said, his voice cold. "*We* can't care for it if you're not *here*."

"I'm visiting with the people. Their animals are dying. Their crops are failing. I'm helping them get fruit for their children. I don't see how my being here—"

"Yes, you're doing so much wandering around the village," Adhiraj interjected. "And in the forest."

It was quiet between them a moment.

"Our kingdom is suffering," Rajan said quietly. "I know that. But I cannot help anyone from *here*."

"All the wells have dried."

"I know."

"Even ours," Adhiraj said.

This surprised Rajan. "*Yours?*"

Adhiraj held his hands open. "I've given all I can give. Now it's your turn to help, Prince Rajan."

"What can I do?" Rajan asked earnestly.

"Start by not wasting every waking hour in the forest, playing like a child."

"I'm not playing like a—"

"I don't care." Adhiraj leaned forward. "I don't care what you're doing, or who you're doing it with. But I do need you here, to do something that will actually help us."

Rajan waited.

Adhiraj sighed heavily. "We have a cousin. A daughter of a noble house, actually. A community west of here, near the great sea. You marry her, we get access to their waters. Their river, and the sea."

Rajan stared at his brother, mouth agape.

"We'll ask for barrels of water for the dowry," Adhiraj said, laughing bitterly and shaking his head. "But once the drought ends it will be even more fruitful. The alliance would give us access to a new trade route, and…" Adhiraj's voice trailed off as he took in his brother's expression.

"I cannot marry her," Rajan said, his eyes fixed on the desk.

Adhiraj's eyes narrowed. "This wouldn't be my first choice for you, either, Bhai. If times were better... I'd rather marry you to someone who could give us real power. But these aren't better times."

"I cannot marry her," Rajan repeated.

"You do know we're in a drought," Adhiraj said slowly.

"I. Can. Not. Marry her," Rajan said, his eyes meeting his brother's.

Adhiraj's jaw tightened. "What do you mean exactly when you say you *can* not?"

Rajan didn't speak.

"You're not saying you *will* not." His eyes narrowed. "You have no noblewoman you're courting. Our late Queen did not arrange a wife for you. I've never heard word of you visiting harems. So when you say you *can* not..."

Neither brother spoke for a long moment.

And then Adhiraj laughed, a harsh, barking sound. "You *can* not. You *can* not? Have you set about giving some woman an illegitimate bastard?"

Rajan's eyes blazed then.

"And there's my answer," Adhiraj said, shaking his head and leaning back.

Rajan cursed himself silently for letting his brother's words affect him enough that his face gave anything away.

"How stupid can you be?" Adhiraj hissed.

Rajan said nothing.

Adhiraj shook his head. "Fine. Do you want us to be rid of her? Or just the baby?"

Rajan looked at him in shock. "What?"

"Do we need to have her killed? Or do you want her brought to the witch woman in town? We can—"

"Enough!" Rajan slammed his fist on the desk in front of him.

Adhiraj raised his brows and sat back in his chair, eyes fixed on his younger brother. "Tsk tsk tsk. No way to speak to your king."

"She is my…" Rajan began, and then froze.

What was he going to say?

That the woman he impregnated is not only *not* noble and *not* from Jaraan—and oh, by the way she lives in the forest—but she is an actual literal goddess?

And, that in fact, she's not just a goddess, but she's the goddess of the river—but she can't do anything about the drought, because inconveniently, none of her river magic seems to be working at the moment.

Rajan realized a very long time had passed since he began speaking, and that his brother was staring at him with a look of irritation.

"Right," Adhiraj said slowly. "I will announce your betrothal tonight in the court. And you can wed in three days time."

Rajan was quiet a long time before he spoke again. "And if I refuse?"

Adhiraj laughed bitterly. "Anything for your king, remember? How can you refuse?"

Rajan shook his head.

"Marry the girl. Serve your people." Adhiraj's voice was cold. "Or leave, and be exiled. And I'll…figure it out. There are other ways."

Rajan swallowed. "What other ways?"

"Ways your gentle heart wouldn't like, Bhai."

Rajan looked away.

"I'll announce it tonight, Rajan, whether you're standing beside me or not. And if you're not here to wed the girl in three days, then…"

Rajan stared into his brother's face, and saw nothing brotherly there.

There was only the exhaustion of a brand new king.

ADHIRAJ WAITED until he knew Rajan was gone before calling in his advisor.

"Pankaj."

"Sahib."

"Your men reported that Rajan has a woman," he said slowly. "In the forest."

"There… have been some reports. Someone thought they saw someone. It may not have been a woman. It may have. Maybe someone saw… Long hair."

"He has a woman."

Pankaj said nothing and kept his gaze averted.

"Send your men, Pankaj. Men who won't question orders."

Pankaj swallowed. "Sahib?"

Adhiraj shook his head. "Maya will be due any day now. My son will be King someday." He took a deep breath. "I don't need some bastard crawling out of a forest in twenty years trying to stake a claim to the house of Jaraan."

Pankaj winced. "Understood, Sahib."

"That will be all, Pankaj."

Pankaj nodded, and left the study.

Adhiraj sat alone, steepling his fingers and staring at the door.

He thought of Rajan's face now.

And of his face when they had been children. Pink cheeks,

long dark curls bouncing against them as their father spun him around.

Thought of their mother wrapping Rajan in an embrace every morning as Adhiraj stood to the side with Pankaj who was already his advisor even when he was still a child. A child who also wanted his father to spin him around, who also wanted his mother to embrace him every morning.

He turned back to his papers.

RAJAN SAT down beside Naga and then lay his head into her lap.

"Adhiraj knows I've been gone. And he knows now about…you. About us."

Naga caressed Rajan's face, his hair. "Well, that's nice. You've decided to tell him we are making a baby together."

Rajan shook his head. "Not exactly, but… he knows anyway."

"Good," Naga said, still stroking his hair.

"He's arranged a marriage for me."

Naga's hand stilled.

Rajan sat up. "With a girl from the western kingdom. A cousin. Their family is noble, something about access to a river… it doesn't matter. I told him no."

Naga smiled. "Good."

"I didn't quite say no," he corrected himself. "But he's announcing it tonight and… it's in three days. If I don't come, he'll exile me… or worse." He swallowed. "And he says if I don't come, he'll do something that… something I won't like. To fix the water problem."

"Something you won't like?" Naga frowned.

"If I know him, he'll probably start a war and take her people's land anyway."

Naga straightened her spine, stretched her neck. "You have three days to marry a woman and possibly save your people from this drought, or you'll be exiled, and possibly start a war. Yes?"

"Yes."

"So then you've come to say goodbye?"

Rajan reached for Naga's hand. "I've come to ask you to run."

Naga smiled. "Oh, but you are full of surprises. Run where?"

"I don't know. Away. Somewhere with water. Somewhere away from Adhiraj."

Naga laughed. "You're just a prince! What will you do if we run far away from your kingdom?"

"I'm educated. I can find work anywhere."

"You'd give up your royalty, your title, the only home you've ever known?"

"I just want to be with you."

Naga narrowed her eyes. "You'd abandon your people to die of thirst? It's children?" She smoothed her long robe. "You'd allow your own child to die of thirst as well?"

Rajan groaned in frustration and threw his hands up. "What would you have me do?"

Naga watched him and said nothing.

Moments passed.

Finally Rajan kicked the ground and sat down heavily on a large rock. "No. I won't abandon the people. I need to solve this somehow."

Naga sat down beside him, nodding. "Good."

"But I can't marry someone else," he said, sighing. "I won't."

"No," Naga agreed. "You've not even married me."

Rajan's eyes grew wide. "Naga, I..." he began, stumbling over the words. "I'll marry you right now, I can do it, let's—"

She caressed his face, shushing him. "Calm yourself, Rajan of Jaraan," she said gently. "I'm a goddess. I know of your devotion."

Rajan exhaled a breath he hadn't realized he was holding.

"How will you save the people?"

He looked down at his hands and shook his head. "I don't know."

"Think."

"The kingdom to the west. I need to travel there. I don't know if their river is even still flowing."

Naga nodded. She said nothing about what she already knew. That their fate was probably no better than this kingdom.

"It's a day's journey, so if I leave now, I can find out if they can help, and come back in time to solve the problem before the wedding."

Naga nodded in encouragement. "Good."

"And then when I've solved the problem, and maybe the rain returns, then we can leave this place anyway. I'll help the people. But then we have to go. We have to go build a life somewhere, together. You and me and our baby."

Naga smiled at him.

Inside, she felt powerless and terrified.

RAJAN RODE out the western kingdom with Bakki.

When he arrived, the girl his brother had promised him to was already dead. The river in their kingdom hadn't seemed to be drying when the marriage had been arranged. But in only days, it had become like a desert.

It was only thanks to the carefully rationed bottles Rajan carried hidden in his coat that he made it back home at all without dying of thirst.

Bakki did not survive.

ON THE DAY Rajan finally returned, Naga had sensed, distantly, people moving through the trees.

Looking for her, perhaps.

But then Rajan returned, and she forgot all about them.

When he came, he told her about the western kingdom before she could ask.

The girl dead. The river gone. Desert in its place. "It's not just us," he whispered.

Naga was silent.

He looked at her then, and she could see him calculating. How many months. How many people.

"Naga." His eyes fixed on the ground. "What if all my people are dead before the baby comes?"

A deep sorrow grew inside Naga at his pain. At her own impotence.

And then he looked up, his eyes suddenly wide. "What about… some other gods? Is there anyone who could—"

Naga's eyes widened.

Her eyes fixed on a distant point in the forest where her river had so recently flowed as she considered the possibility.

"Could you?" His eyes were wide. "Is there someone who could help?"

"I… maybe. But don't know if it's wise," she said slowly. "For me to call my siblings here."

"Naga." Rajan pleaded. "You have to do whatever you can."

She stared at him helplessly.

And considered what this might cost them.

PART TWO
MORTALS

CHOICES

In the morning, Naga waited until Rajan left before she moved east of her river, to a large clearing illuminated by the sun, and called for her siblings.

"Aag…" she called, her voice low. "Zamīn… Havaa." She looked around. "Raat. Din."

There was a long, long moment when Naga wondered if this was madness. If they could even do anything about the drought in the first place. If they would even come at her beckoning.

If they were even listening.

Din and Raat appeared first. "Hello Behen," they said in greeting.

Zamīn arrived—and avoided Naga's eyes. And then Havaa arrived, and took a step toward Naga—but then seemed to stop herself.

And before Naga could ask anything, Aag appeared.

"Hello, Naga," he said with a broad smile. "Finally remembered us?"

"I've called you all to ask for your help."

Aag laughed. "*Our* help? What can we help you with?"

Naga looked down at her hands. "I can't seem…" she cleared her throat. "I need your help. The mortals need water, and… I need your help."

"Isn't water your area, Naga?" Aag asked.

Naga swallowed. "Yes. But… maybe I'm ill. Some kind of mortal affliction…" her voice trailed off, and she checked to make sure her robes were tied loosely around her middle, concealing her belly.

"You think the droughts are… your fault?" Aag had a funny look on his face.

Naga said nothing.

"Living among mortals has made *you* beneath yourself." Aag spoke slowly. "No, Naga. Mortal afflictions cannot suppress the goddess of water."

He took a step closer to her, his heat radiating to her body, filling her with warmth.

And fear.

She looked up at him. The blazing golden eyes. The large frame that, in her mortal body, towered over her.

"It's been me," he said softly, almost touching her. "I've been drying your rivers. Burning your clouds. Stopping your rains." A pause. "Did you really think anything mortal could suppress you?"

Naga couldn't breathe.

"You," she began.

Something shifted in his face. "If you didn't know," he said slowly, "then why did you call us here?"

Naga froze.

"If she thought she was simply impotent due to some mortal-world induced problem, then she *would* think she'd need all of our help," Din mused.

"But none of us can create water," Raat interjected.

"None of us alone can create her element, but we—the five of us *together*—could create it," Zamīn said slowly.

"But why would she think something mortal had robbed her of it?" Raat frowned. "What mortal affliction could—"

Havaa gasped and her eyes met Naga's.

Naga swallowed, her eyes silently pleading for Havaa to say nothing.

A moment passed.

"What is it?" Aag demanded.

Havaa's eyes lingered on Naga, concern apparent on her face. "Naga..."

And then it was Zamīn who spoke next. "Ohhhh." She nodded. "You are with child."

A strange sound escaped Aag then as he stumbled back from Naga. Din laughed at that same moment, muffling it.

Havaa's eyes widened and went to Aag.

"Oh, but that is foolish!" Raat cackled.

"A half *mortal* child?" Aag blurted out in astonishment. "Are you insane?"

"And you thought this would suppress your powers," Zamīn said, frowning at Naga. "But surely you remember the Great Goddess—" she trailed off as she noticed Aag's glowering gaze.

Aag turned from Zamīn to Naga.

"I'll make you an offer," he said. "I'll end the droughts. The rain returns tonight. Every well, every river, every crop, restored. Thousands of lives for one."

A desperation filled Naga. She looked up at him, waiting for the rest.

"And in exchange, I get to kill your mortal."

Naga's eyes went wide.

Aag watched her expression. "Or, you have another

choice," he said. "You can choose your mortal. Save him, and your… half-mortal baby," his lip curled in disgust. "And come home now. Forfeit the wager. Flood the earth and leave the rest of the mortals to die."

In this mortal form, the heat radiating from Aag was no longer warmth. It felt like burning.

It was Zamīn who stepped forward now voice measured: "Behen, your mortal… he is just mortal. He's already lived more than two decades. He has—what? Five decades remaining? Six? To doom so many mortals and save just one is foolishness."

Naga thought of the battlefields then. Of mortals lying dead. Of the heat she could feel, rising from flames with no source.

"We had. A wager." Naga said, her voice measured. "One that I've nearly won."

Aag's eyes went blank. "And we still do."

"You've been interfering. You've been killing mortals. You've been drying my clouds, my rivers?"

"I have," Aag agreed.

"These were not the terms of our wager."

"They were not," Aag agreed.

"The terms of our agreement were–"

"I'm changing them," he said flatly. "I'm a god. I can do that."

They both felt it as he spoke the words. Vows spoken by gods were not changed without consequence. The mortal world, the ground beneath their feet, the fabric of time and space and stars and sky, all resisting the change.

Cursing this very place with the weight of this violation.

But Aag did what he wanted.

"Come home now and save your mortal, killing everyone

else." He smiled coldly. "Or save everyone else, and watch me kill your mortal."

"Why?" Naga asked softly.

For a moment, something raw flickered across Aag's face. "Because you were supposed to come back," he said, voice a growl. "You were supposed to realize they're nothing. Instead you've been down here for over nine hundred years, and you look at this mortal the way you used to—"

Naga was frozen in place. She thought of her rainclouds, then. Destruction was how he loved.

Aag's jaw tightened. "This is what you want?" he said, his voice quieter now. "To be adored by a creature who will be ashes before you've finished a single thought?"

Naga watched as he began to wave the other siblings away. Zamīn's eyes locked on Raat's and the two disappeared together first. Din followed, looking irritated.

Only Havaa remained, and took a step toward Naga. But Aag's eyes moved to her, and then she, too, was gone.

Naga said nothing.

"I am your equal," he said. "I am the only one who has ever been your equal. And you choose to be worshipped by something beneath you?"

"His worship," she said quietly, "is what makes him worthy of me."

Something crossed Aag's face. "He isn't me."

"No," she agreed. "He isn't."

"Call me when you're ready," he said, stepping back. And then he was gone.

AFTER THEY VANISHED, Naga stood in the dry riverbed, frozen.

She could stay. Let Aag kill Rajan. End the drought and save thousands.

She could forfeit the wager and return home. Save Rajan and the baby, and drown everyone else.

She looked down at her hands, where the ghost of blue patterns appeared briefly, before fading away.

For another day, and another night, she remained frozen in place.

RAJAN CAME THAT NIGHT, and she was still standing in the same spot.

"Naga? Have you been out here all day?" And then he saw her face and froze. "What's wrong?"

"Nothing," she said, swallowing, forcing a smile. "Come here, Rajan of Jaraan."

He climbed down into the dry riverbed and took her hands. His lips were cracked. The palace stores had dried.

"Never mind," he said softly. "Your siblings?"

She nodded, wincing.

"Will they help?"

She did not reply.

"Naga." His voice was firm. "Will they help?"

She met his eyes. "This *is* them," she said flatly. "The drought."

His eyes went wide. "What do you mean?"

"I mean my... *brother*. He is causing the drought. He is suppressing my power." She laughed bitterly. "He offered me a choice. He wants something from me that I... can't... give."

"What?"

"He wants me to come home. And he wants the mortal

world to flood." She did not add that this would spare Rajan's life.

His eyes widened. "Why would he do that?"

She clenched her jaw, the truth spilling from her before she could stop herself saying it. "Because he is jealous. Because he wishes he had claim over me. Because he wishes I were his lover."

Rajan nearly stumbled back. He was silent.

"And I have never wanted any of that," Naga added. "And it kills him… To see me with… you."

Rajan was quiet.

"So he wants you to come home," he said slowly. "But you said he offered you a choice. What was the choice?"

"If I returned home now, it would be a violation of a wager we made nearly a thousand years ago," she said evasively.

"Yes, but what choice did he offer? You said he offered you some choice."

She twisted the fabric of her robe. "I can return home, and the mortal world… floods. Everyone dies. Except for you."

"But why would he spare *me*? You just said he's jealous. What does sparing me…" And then Rajan's eyes went wide. "He knows you would never choose to kill everyone." He swallowed. "What's the other choice?"

She closed her eyes tightly.

"Naga. What is the other choice?"

She bit her lip to stop it quivering. "The other option is… He kills you," she said. "And the rain—" She stopped.

Rajan understood immediately. "Naga," he began softly.

"No," she hissed. "No," she gasped, a strangled sound of panic, and froze in place, horrified at the *humanness* of her feelings.

Her eyes fixed on Rajan as her breathing quickened, her pulse accelerating.

Rajan pulled her close.

"No," she repeated.

"Alright," he said, trying to soothe her, wrapping his arms around her, even while trying to still his hands from shaking. "Alright."

CHAPTER 8
FLAMES

That night, Rajan didn't sleep. He lay and watched Naga.

The rise and fall of her chest as she slept. The curl of her hair, a long tendril resting on her throat. A slender hand resting on the curve of her belly.

What if he hadn't come to the forest that morning? He reached forward to touch her face. *What if his mortal life had passed him by without ever knowing her?*

Long before morning, Rajan was gone.

And when Naga woke, she found in his place the small blue stone she had given him. She picked it up, turning it over in her hand.

And she knew immediately where he had gone.

The clearing to the east.

And knew, too, that by the time she reached it, it would be too late.

～

AT THE EDGE OF A CLEARING, three men crouched, watching Rajan waking up beside a woman, reaching forward to touch her face. They had been hiding in wait for hours.

They watched as he finally left her.

Unprotected.

Even in the low morning light filtered through the tree canopy, even lying down, they could see she was the most beautiful woman any of them had laid eyes on.

Her long curling hair. The smooth, glowing curve of her face.

Even lying down, they could see the curve of her womb.

"I think… I think she is pregnant," the youngest of the three whispered to his companions.

"What of it," the man beside him, with a thick mustache, hissed. "You *heard* Pankaj. Find Rajan's woman. Kill her. Or do not return."

"We cannot kill her—we'll be cursed," the youngest man hissed back. "Our children's children will be cursed."

"We have a job to do," the oldest of the three said. "We cannot return with nothing." He began to rise, but the youngest man took a step backward.

"I can't kill a pregnant woman," he repeated.

"Fine," said the oldest. "I'll do it myself."

But then the earth shuddered beneath their feet. They heard something thundering to the east, and turned in the direction of the sound.

And by the time they turned back to where Rajan and the woman had been lying, the woman was already gone.

The men began running in the direction of the noise, arriving at a clearing where Prince Rajan stood, speaking up to the sky.

～

Rajan's voice rang out across the forest. "Gods! Siblings of Naga! I offer myself willingly. End the drought. Spare my people."

For a moment, there was nothing.

And then the smell of the air changed to that of wet earth and burning wood, and somehow also like the smell of the earth after a lightning storm. The light faded briefly, and then the temperature surged.

And then a crack of thunder.

And then, Aag descended, breaking through the sky surrounded by tendrils of fire licking at his face, curling tenderly around his arms like Naga's snakes. The heat radiating from him felt more like the heat from a fire than the heat of a summer's day.

His feet touched the ground and it scorched black. "Ah, the mortal has some sense," the god of fire said languidly.

Hidden from the clearing, in the underbrush along the tree-line, three men stood completely still, mouths agape.

Not one of them moved a muscle.

"Take me, and spare my kingdom, and all the kingdoms beyond it," Rajan said, his voice as steady as he could make it despite his trembling. "I offer myself willingly. Save my people."

"Gladly," Aag smiled. "But I'd like to hear why."

"Because I—" Rajan stood taller. "I love her. Let me make this sacrifice, and you'll leave my kingdom. And all the kingdoms... alone. Do we have an accord?"

Aag was quiet a moment. He looked at the mortal.

This small, trembling, brave thing that was so beneath him. So beneath Naga.

But for just a moment, Aag saw the bravery in his trembling. And understood what it was Naga saw.

Aag pushed forward a slow line of fire, inching closer to

the mortal without touching him. It formed a thin circle of flames that trapped him where he stood, rising and curling in a cruel dance.

And with a casual flick Rajan's wrists were bound.

At the edge of the clearing, the three men watched in horror.

Aag cocked his head to the side. "I think my sister should witness this moment, don't you? She's so fond of mortal bravery."

Rajan's eyes grew wide.

"*Behen*," Aag now called.

The word carried through the forest like smoke, drawing her nearer.

And it was then that Naga made her way to the edge of the clearing, suspicion turning to horror as she saw Rajan standing before her brother.

Wrists bound, trapped in a circle of flames.

"No—" she screamed, lunging forward, before she slammed into invisible bars.

"What have you done?" she screamed. The bars were Aag's heat, pressed into the shape of a cage, and they burned where she touched them in a way her mortal skin had never burned. But it was Raat and Din whose laughter she could feel, rather than hear, as she rattled the bars despite the searing pain

Men—her own brothers—caged her in.

"Your mortal made a choice," Aag said. "Since you couldn't."

Rajan's eyes met hers across the clearing, through the smoke and the flames.

His lips formed words: *Forgive me.*

She threw herself against the bars. "Rajan, no—"

For the briefest moment—a heartbeat—the bars seemed

almost to break, to dissolve into water, a splash hitting the scorched earth at Rajan's feet, making a sizzling sound, and Naga felt that hum of power again—

And then Aag's heat slammed back down. The cage sealed, and Naga was powerless once more.

"Your silence was your answer, Naga." Aag said gently. "You couldn't choose. So your mortal chose for you." He turned to Rajan with a smile. "We both did."

"Aag, please—" Naga's voice cracked.

Aag continued to speak, his voice flat. "And your mortal made the right choice, Behen. He chose to save thousands. He chose nobly."

Rajan's eyes flickered to Naga's stomach—just briefly. When his eyes met hers again, they were wet.

"You wanted to know what mortality felt like? This is it. Helplessness. Watching what you love die while you can do nothing." His voice dropped. "But I'm giving you a kindness. A chance to say goodbye."

And then the ring of fire burned brighter, and the smell in the air turned to iron and rain and flames.

A sob broke loose from Naga's lips as her eyes fixed on Rajan's.

In the tree-line, three hidden men sat immobilized. Not one of them breathed.

The light changed quickly from dawn to dusk, and then to gold, and then to a color that was like lightning—a color that the three men in the tree-line would never be able to name.

And then, Aag turned to Rajan and smiled.

And Rajan's body burst into flames that briefly, for only a moment, lit the entire forest a brilliant and blinding white.

And then there was nothing at all.

CHAPTER 9
FLOODS

The cage dissolved the moment Rajan's body hit the ground.

And in the clearing, Naga fell to her knees.

And somewhere deep in the mortal earth, in the waters that still flowed deep under its surface, something began to surge.

Something pushing and rising up through the earth, and through every cloud, and through every stream and river he had dried.

It felt distinctly like *Naga*.

And Aag realized his hold over her power—his heat, his drying—had broken. He could no longer contain her.

He saw it, then.

Naga's face contorting in an image of rage.

Of grief.

And he understood. There was no taking this back. There would be no forgiveness for this.

Naga, a vision of unspeakable pain, began to scream.

And then—

Above, the sky opened, and rain began to fall. Thunder

and lightning and torrential rains fell all around, everywhere, in all places.

Aag could not dry these rainclouds.

He stumbled back, retreating to his fortress, pulling in his heat from all sides as the truth of what he had done settled into him.

NAGA WAS SCREAMING STILL, but didn't know where the sound was coming from. Didn't understand that it came from somewhere deep inside her mortal body.

She cradled Rajan's body as rain fell all around them.

Absently, distantly, she noticed the water was soaking her hair, her skin, and mixing with Rajan's blood beneath her hands.

Goddess and mortal.

Alive and dead.

Her spare hand still clutched her stomach. Their child still moved inside her.

Alive, for now.

She laid Rajan's body gently on the ground and looked up into the rain.

"Aag," she growled, her voice carrying across realms to Aag's ears, "Hear me now, Aag. I will never forgive you, Aag. You will only ever know solitude."

And then, Naga pressed her palm to the earth.

For one heartbeat, she did nothing.

And then she pulled.

And immediately, her power coursed through her mortal body, through her womb, through her arms and hands and fingers and into the earth itself, vibrating out from her body into the very air.

The raindrops froze in midair.

And then they flowed back up.

Rivers reversed course.

Oceans rose.

Every body of water on earth answered her call.

Mortal villages began to flood. She felt them: mortal lives in peril, at risk of being swept away.

No.

She did not lose the wager. She would *not* drown the mortals. She would not harm the people Rajan had died to save.

No. Her flood would drown the dwellings of the gods.

She forced the waters to obey, her powers coursing through her now. She directed the rain, the rivers, the oceans, to those places where the gods, her siblings, lived.

Zamīn's caves collapsed as water carved channels through their walls, destroyed their foundations. The twins' sky-palaces fell, pulled down by rain that wouldn't stop. At Havaa's wind-temples, Naga hesitated—but only briefly—before letting the water sweep them away.

And Aag's fire-mountain fortress first began to shake under the weight of torrential rain, and then slowly turned to mud.

When it was finished, when she knew in her very bones that her siblings' sanctuaries had been destroyed by her power, that they would retreat to their other, higher realm, far and far away from this mortal place, only then did she stop.

Only then did she finally let the rain fall back down onto the earth at her feet, and the rivers to flow back into their banks, and the oceans and seas to return to their floors.

Only then did she let herself fall back down to the flooded earth beside Rajan.

Somewhere in the distant underbrush, three men were running. One, the oldest, slipped in the mud, and smashed his head on a large rock, dying instantly.

Another, the shorter mustached man, was swept into a river that was raging and rising violently at his side.

The youngest of the three was still on his feet, running. He would not stop until he reached the road.

Finally on the wet earth next to Rajan's body, Naga screamed and screamed until she didn't know when her screaming had become weeping.

And then she wrapped Rajan's body in her arms.

He was still warm.

She screamed as she held him, rocking his body against hers, her tears mixing with rain, rain with tears.

She held him and rocked him a long time, until finally she thought she had no more tears left, and she laid him back down on the wet earth.

But she did have more tears. And she wept, and wept, and wept.

Soon, the snakes came.

First three, then seven, then a hundred and more arrived, slithering closer and closer until they surrounded Rajan's body.

She wept as the snakes wrapped him, and as they absorbed him, and as they made him a part of their skin.

She wept until the earth beneath her, the earth beneath where Rajan's body had been, and where the snakes had made him a part of them, was all water—all sorrow.

She wept as the snakes slowly withdrew, their scales shining with her tears.

And then the last snake left behind a single tooth in the place where Rajan had been.

Naga picked it up.

And her free hand went to her stomach, where a mortal heartbeat and the power of the gods still existed, intertwined.

Blue patterns blazed suddenly across her hands, coiling up her arms, her throat.

And finally, she stopped weeping.

Naga moved through the forest slowly. In a daze.

She passed the places where she had once made love to Rajan of Jaraan.

And she watched as everything around her, tree branches, leaves, insects, seemed to draw away from her, as if afraid of her. Of her grief.

The child inside of her moved.

She closed her eyes.

Mortal heartbeat and divine power, still intertwined. The only piece of Rajan of Jaraan she still had.

Still alive.

She tilted her face up to the rain and felt the drops on her mortal skin, one by one, until they stopped.

CHAPTER 10

IMPERMANENCE

One day Naga awoke to feel the pain that meant her child would soon come. And she felt utterly alone.

And the pain and the aloneness began to grow, and they gave way to fury, and violence, and then, to absolute power.

And she began to push.

She felt the pain of her child's coming in every corner of her being, felt pain that was unlike every other pain.

She yelled from a place that came from inside of her womb, a place that came from the source of her very being, and as she yelled, she pushed.

She yelled and pushed, and yelled and pushed, alone, in the forest, through water and through blood and through fear. And she screamed and she pushed—and she made life.

And then—

A daughter.

And then her daughter cried, and the river rose in response, and Naga wrapped the baby in her arms and pulled her to her breast, and when the baby began to suckle, Naga cried in exhaustion, and in relief.

She looked down. Her daughter's eyes were dark, and plain, and mortal. They were Rajan's eyes.

She named her Anitya.

ANITYA HAD LIVED for hardly an hour before Naga first had the thought that filled her with a dread so deep she nearly caused a flood:

Anitya was only half god.

Which meant Anitya would someday die.

HAVAA CAME ONCE, when Anitya was still an infant.

She appeared at the river's edge, looking unlike herself. Diminished, somehow. Un-godlike.

"Naga," she called.

Havaa was the first person, mortal or god—besides Anitya—whose voice Naga had heard since Aag killed Rajan.

Naga held her daughter closer.

"I've come…" Havaa's voice shook. "To say I'm sorry."

The breeze picked up, lifting Anitya's hair. She giggled, reaching for the wind.

Naga said nothing for a long time.

"Naga?" Havaa asked softly.

Naga shook her head. "Why didn't you stop him?"

"I know." Havaa's eyes filled with tears. "I should have—"

"You should have been brave. You should have chosen me."

The wind died.

"I did choose you," Havaa whispered. "They didn't…

they trapped me. Somewhere outside of time. I didn't even know until it was done." Her eyes spilled over. "I don't speak to Aag anymore. Or the twins."

Naga stared out into the distance for a long moment. And she knew Havaa was speaking the truth.

She looked down at her daughter, who was still batting her hands, searching again for the breeze.

"Her name is Anitya," she said finally, meeting Havaa's eyes.

And then, through her tears, Havaa let out a laugh, before stopping herself.

And then she laughed again.

And then Naga started to laugh too. And soon they were both, sisters and oldest friends, laughing with such abandon that they seemed to forget where they were or what had passed between them.

As soon as one of them would slow down, the other would screech with a laugh and the other would dissolve all over again.

They laughed for so long that Anitya began to cry.

Havaa slowed then, wiping at her tears. "Not subtle," she said finally.

Naga bit back a smile, warding off another fit of laughing.

"Anitya," Havaa whispered, sending a cool wind swirling around the baby. Anitya squealed with delight.

Naga took a deep breath, looking into her sister's eyes then. "You can visit," she said finally. "But only you."

Havaa nodded. But then added, "Zamīn wants to come see—"

"No," Naga interrupted. "Only you."

Soon after, Havaa left.

∾

BUT THE NEXT time Havaa came, Zamīn was walking behind her. Naga's eyes shot to Havaa's in betrayal, but Zamīn held up her hand.

"Before you speak, Behen," Zamīn said quietly, "know that my power will always be greater than our youngest sister's."

Havaa looked away in shame.

"I know that," Naga said quietly. "I also know they trapped her. But they couldn't have trapped you."

Zamīn did not object.

"You knew what he was doing," Naga said quietly, but her eyes fixed on Zamīn's. "And you knew Raat and Din were helping him."

Zamīn still said nothing.

"You don't deny it?"

Zamīn sighed. "I did not stop them," she agreed. "But only because…" She cleared her throat. "I did not understand. What the mortal meant to you."

Naga said nothing.

"But I've come to give glad news," Zamīn went on. "Half-mortal children live… exceptionally long lives. Much longer than normal mortals."

Naga still didn't look at her, but something inside Naga unknotted then. Something that had been tightening with every passing day since Anitya's birth.

Finally, Naga nodded at Zamīn.

"I wish her a long life," Zamīn said, nodding at the child.

And then she was gone.

And Havaa's eyes were full of apology. Naga sighed and reached out for her younger sister, who came close and sat at her side.

～

ZAMIN NEVER RETURNED after that day, but Havaa still came sometimes. She never stayed long.

Just brought breezes for Anitya to play with and sat with Naga as she raised her daughter, the way that family does.

WHEN HER DAUGHTER was old enough to walk, Naga brought her to the forest where Rajan had died.

Where a sapling now grew from scorched earth. She knelt and placed her hands on the ground.

Aag's fire had gone into this ground. The sapling should not have survived. But then, Rajan's blood had also gone into this ground. And so had Naga's tears.

Something had taken root here, that even fire could not burn away.

"I'm going to build you something," Naga whispered. She spoke to her daughter, but she also spoke to the ground, and to the sapling, and to its roots, and to the blood of Rajan of Jaraan that she knew was embedded in the earth beneath her.

She touched the sapling before her gently, before pressing her palm to the dirt, thinking of Zamīn, who had made this dirt and all other dirt like it.

She put a second hand to the ground, thinking of Havaa as a breeze cooled her skin.

She closed her eyes and thought of her younger brothers, Din and Raat, and imagined nights turning to days turning to nights, as the sun rose and set over a thick, tall tree that would grow from this earth some day.

And then her jaw tightened as she thought of Aag.

She felt warmth beneath her palms—heat radiating from deep in the earth, deep enough that the fire at the belly of this world would have to reshape itself to allow it… and she felt it: a temple growing far below her palms, far beneath the soil.

"Mama?" Her daughter whispered.

Naga knew: This kind of power, power that pulled against the powers of other gods, came with a price.

She didn't care. She pressed down into the earth and tears stung her eyes as she murmured the words under her breath.

Awakened may enter.

Naga imagined Anitya coming to this place someday with her own daughter.

The sleeping may not.

Her eyes narrowed as she thought of her eldest brother. And in that moment, she knew: creating this place would bind part of her divine essence here forever. She would never again return to the god realm. She would never again be what she once was.

The mouth exacts its price.

And then, she thought of how much she had loved Rajan. She thought of how it felt to see him die. How when he had died, the world—her world—had ended.

And then she thought of how it felt now, to have her daughter at her side. And she closed her eyes tight.

In death, reborn.

And then the earth rumbled beneath her feet, and her eyes flew open.

Beneath them, she knew, the earth—the future—was changing. She reached for Anitya, holding her close, looking into her wide, dark eyes and whispering sounds of comfort. But inside, she felt the thrill of divine creation. This one last creation.

She looked back to the sapling.

At last, she had made something permanent.

ANITYA GREW.

When she was five, she found a snake near the river. She held it in her hands, caressing it tenderly. Naga watched her holding the snake and thought of snakes shedding skin.

When she was 16, she spent more time among the mortals of the kingdom of Jaraan.

She brought news regularly to her mother, who spent her time still in forests and rivers and underground places. News of schools for boys and a temple for the girls, and news of King Adhiraj, and of his handsome son Rajvir, who was prince of Jaraan and was now nearly a man, and who Anitya said had eyes like hers.

When Anitya was 19, she met a mortal man in the kingdom of Jaraan. He was a weaver's son.

When Anitya married him, Naga gave her the small, blueish stone to keep with her, always.

Anitya had children of her own and a new world began.

In her spare time, she kept her mother company.

And like her mother before her, when her children grew older, she brought them to the Mouth.

From a distance, Naga watched the kingdom change.

Watched as King Adhiraj grew old.

He had fed his people after the drought. Built roads and new aqueducts. And as kings do, he tired, and grew old and weary, and one day, died.

And then Adhiraj's son Rajvir, a boy who was half Jaraan and half Daraio, became King.

Naga watched as Rajvir established something called the Covenant.

And she felt the change in the water. The dilution of her power.

Anitya felt it too, in the way her daughters' daughters were taught to be quiet in market. Taught to be still in temple. Taught to be careful in ways she had never had to be.

Naga felt it again when a granddaughter came to the river —a girl with those deep, dark eyes—sitting at the bank, her hand swirling through the water. She felt it when she heard a low voice—her brother? Her father?—call her away. Felt it when the girl did not return.

She watched as some of her line became travelers, unwilling to stay under the shifting rules of Jaraan. Watched them leave, always along rivers, carrying the knowledge of the water, and of magic, and of Naga herself, and every few generations, return again. Their daughters, too, traveled, left, returned, left again.

She also watched those who stayed. And saw that fewer and fewer of them came to the forest or the river.

As Naga's bloodline—Rajan's bloodline—spread, the world around the descendants changed into something Naga no longer recognized.

92

Thankfully, she did not have to watch it all alone. Zamīn had been right; Anitya did live much longer than normal mortals.

Naga watched Anitya as she watched her children's children enter the world. Watched her own daughters become mothers, and then grandmothers. Watched Anitya grieve her husband, and then her own daughters, and then their daughters after them. Watched with Anitya as generation after generation, flickered past.

The world ended all the time.

Anitya began to show signs of old age only after so many daughters of daughters of daughters had come and gone that she could hardly remember who each was.

And it was only then that Naga allowed herself to consider what she would do when Anitya's life, too, burned away.

NAGA HELD her as she passed, the way she had held Rajan.

A snake came.

It coiled itself at Anitya's feet, and stayed for a long time. And when the last breath left her, the snake left, too.

This wasn't like losing Rajan.

There was no rage this time to distract her. There was only grief: the price of love.

Before Anitya, she had experienced the multitudes of the universe, infinite, stretching in all directions. She had experienced all of that before Rajan, too, but it was different from losing Anitya.

With Anitya, there had been so much of everything. Anitya *was* infinity.

After Anitya…

Nothing in the universe, not even being a goddess, could have prepared her for life after her daughter.

IN THE YEARS THAT FOLLOWED, this grief would rush out of her in the form of a flood, destroying a town here, drowning a village there.

Some great-granddaughter somewhere would die, and it would remind her of losing Anitya, and then before she even realized what had happened, her rivers of tears would have already left behind a wave of destruction.

She always found a way to harness the flood, to rein in the destruction, to regain her control—but not before damage was already done.

And in these flooding years, every time Naga cried, somewhere very far away, Aag would feel her grief.

And something—not guilt exactly, but perhaps the knowledge of his role in Naga's sorrow—would shake him to his core.

And then the earth, too, would shake.

Wells dried, crops failed, and Aag's own sorrow became a consequence for the earth. Many mortals died.

Impermanence.

CHAPTER II

TRANSFORMATION

After Anitya, Naga was a shell of who she had been. She grieved for a long time.

And then one day, she laughed. She had remembered the day she had first shown Rajan eternity in her mouth—his awe, his wonder… and she was laughing.

And as she laughed, and as she remembered, she opened her mouth wide.

Wider than she should have been able to.

She expanded her jaw until her mouth was impossibly large, and contained everything within it.

And then she breathed in: the air, the dirt, the sky itself, the stars, the sunshine, heat from distant fires, the entire river —she inhaled it all.

And in the next breath, she exhaled—

And her mortal form was gone.

～

THE RIVER WAS inside Naga now. The water should have drowned her mortal form. Instead, it cradled her, womb-like.

Time unraveled.

She remembered the pain. The mortal form in which she had loved Rajan, and birthed Anitya, and felt the crushing weight of losing them both.

She wanted to forget. To be free of that grief.

But she also wanted to remember forever.

She wanted both.

Once, she had created this river, and made it her home. Now, she would unburden herself. She would fill the river with her memories, and her pain, and her love, and her grief, and let her mind rest.

And she would become the river.

She would flow between her own consciousness, and the water itself, again, and back again, visiting with her memories when she longed to, and becoming water when she longed to.

And she would let the river become her, too.

Naga felt her mortal body dissolving and reforming.

God becoming water, water becoming god.

Naga became the river, and the river became Naga.

Once again, Naga was water.

THE MEHR'AN TELL many stories about what happened next.

In some versions of the story, after her beloved was taken, the river goddess became the river itself.

In others, she became the serpent mother: a protector and a destroyer.

But in the oldest stories, they're the same: The river is the serpent, and the serpent is the goddess who shed her skin and became water.

The Mehr'an people—a traveling people—believe the river goddess chose certain bloodlines to carry her power, and that she waits in the river, guarding what remains of her line. Protecting the people. Protecting the women.

The Covenant, too, tell their own stories. They claim that the women in the kingdom of Jaraan had begun to rebel against the natural order, to forget their husbands and children.

They claim those women went out in search of something in the forests and rivers, and that some came back with magic, and selfishnesses, and greed for freedoms over which they had no claim.

And then, they claim, the waters rose to punish them. To teach them lessons—The Flooding Years.

But this much is true:

Naga's daughters returned, again and again, to the temple she had created; to the Mouth of the Serpent.

And when their daughters came of age, they brought them to the Mouth, as their mothers before them had done. And again, and again.

Daughters emerged with patterns coiling like snakes around their arms, like flames around their bodies, like swirls marking the currents of the river.

But not all daughters entered. Some stood at the threshold and turned back, leaving only with what their blood carried. Still others were born with the patterns of Naga's power, yet never felt the call to enter the mouth.

And some daughters just stayed away because home was Jaraan and its Covenant.

The daughters began to come less frequently.

And after a time, the Mouth—or perhaps Naga herself in some way—grew tired, and began to close itself.

Still, sometimes a daughter would come, and now, Naga would demand proof: a price—a deer, a bird, an elder ready to end her time on the mortal world, or a snake—especially a snake.

And then, the Mouth would rumble happily, and reveal stone steps, welcoming the daughter home.

As time went on, hardly anyone at all came to the Mouth of the Serpent.

Most of the women born in the town of Jaraan knew nothing of its history. Knew nothing of a time when women made up the royal council, or of a time when Queen Rajni of Jaraan ruled, knew nothing of old gods, or of even Naga herself.

And so, as the people forgot, Naga let herself begin to forget.

She stopped spending time in her body. Instead, she spent more and more time flowing as the river itself, into streams, into rainfall, into tears that fell from the eyes of women scorned by lovers or fathers or brothers or priests or other kinds of liars. Into the very blood of the people of this land.

And she waited for the day that one of them would remember what flowed in their blood.

Waited for the day that one of them would make her remember what she had once been.

She waited a very long time.

Until one day, a girl with amber eyes came to the water and remembered.

ACKNOWLEDGMENTS

I want to thank my kids: Naveen—who is always the first person who asks questions about my stories, and without whom I'd never have written the story of the river goddess, and Ishaan, who is always creating something and reminds me daily to keep making. Thank you to my husband David for being my partner in thinking (and in life). Thank you to my mom Sonia, for continuing to read everything I write.

A special thanks to Sarah Khan Azamy for being in my corner and for the art that brought Jaraan to life, and to my friends who cheered me on alongside her. Thank you to the early readers and ARC readers who gave this story their time and attention and love.

As always, I am thankful for the legacy of storytelling that has been passed down in my family. The saakhis and legends and the folk stories I was raised on are why I am still obsessed with stories now.

Thank you to everyone who has supported The River's Daughter and made it possible for me to keep writing in this universe. You are why I now have an alternate universe in my head where stories from Jaraan won't stop growing—this story started as a tiny seed of an idea, and like Sahira's story, it just kept growing.

Thank you, most of all, to you, the reader of Naga's story. Whether you found this story first or came here after *The River's Daughter*—thank you for stepping into this world, and for following the river back to where it began.

THE GODS

Naga
Goddess of Water
In the First Age, Naga was water. Her nature is fluidity, change, evolution
—but also depth and rage. She contains everything, and belongs to no
place.

Aag
God of Fire
The eldest and most consuming of the siblings, Aag is fire at the heart of
the earth… sustaining warmth and destructive fury. He watches from his
fortress in the fire-mountain, and what he cannot have, he burns.

Havaa
Goddess of Wind
The most tender of the siblings, Havaa breathed air into the world and
into the mortals themselves. She resides in wind-temples that move
where she wills them.

Zamīn
Goddess of Earth
Zamīn rules the earth itself. She carved the earth's caverns and tunnels.
Hers is the most measured and grounded voice among the siblings.

The Twins: Raat & Din
Twin Gods of Night and Day
Locked in an eternal tug-of-war between shadow and light are the
youngest of the divine siblings: Raat (night) and Din (day). Together, they
are chaos.

The Great Goddess
The Creator of All Worlds
The matriarch of the gods who call themselves siblings. She made the
gods, and made them answerable to her, though not always obedient.

A Note from the Author

Thank you for reading *The River Goddess*, the origin story of the river, and everything it carries. Naga's story is also the story of Sahira's bloodline, and the beginning of everything that will unfold in the town of Jaraan.

If you'd like more stories from Jaraan, as well as early access to bonus scenes and future releases, please join here:

PUNITARICE.COM/NEWSLETTER

Continue the story in *The River's Daughter*

The River's Daughter is a lush romantic mythic fantasy of forbidden love, awakening power, and what it costs to remember who you are…

(Available everywhere books are sold)

ABOUT THE AUTHOR

Dr. Punita Rice is a former education researcher and teacher, and the author of *Brown Voices: South Asian American Experiences in Schools*, a book on South Asian Americans' retrospective reflections on their K–12 experiences. *The River's Daughter* is her mythic fantasy of forbidden love, resistance, and river magic, and is inspired by the Punjabi legend of Mirza Sahiba. It is an Amazon #1 Bestseller in Asian Myth & Legend and Top 10 Fantasy Bestseller. *The River Goddess* is its standalone prequel, a gods and mortals story of love, loss, and where the river's power began.

instagram.com/punitarice
facebook.com/punitarice
tiktok.com/@punitarice

www.ingramcontent.com/pod-product-compliance
Lightning Source LLC
Chambersburg PA
CBHW062231150726
47991CB00006B/2535